Sports heROES

extreme sports

Other Books in the Sports Heroes Series

extreme sports

Mark Littleton

Zonderkidz

Zonder**kidz**™

The children's group of Zondervan

www.zonderkidz.com

Sports Heroes: Extreme Sports
Copyright © 2002 by Mark Littleton

Requests for information should be addressed to:
Grand Rapids, Michigan 49530

ISBN: 0–310–70293–3

Editor: *Barbara Scott*
Art direction: *Lisa Workman*
Cover design: *Alan Close*
Cover photography: *Simon Cudby*
Interior design: *Todd Sprague*
Interior photography: *Allsport, Jay Haizlip / Get a Grip, Jorge Visser / jhvisser@infowest.com, Mike Isler / islerphoto, Pierre Tostee / tostee.com, and Steve Allen / Frogman Foto / 3069 Diablo View Rd. / Pleasant Hill, CA 94523 / (925) 256-4678*

Printed in the United States of America

02 03 04 05 06 07 /❖DC/ 10 9 8 7 6 5 4 3 2 1

*To Jeanette, Nicole, Alisha, and Gardner—
the family that keeps me going.
Much thanks for help on this book
from Robyne Baker,
who got me excellent research and interviews;
Dave Branon of Sports Spectrum magazine,
for his suggestions;
and Allan Palmeri of Sharing the Victory,
for his help and suggestions.
Also, thanks to my publisher at Zonderkidz,
Gary Richardson, and my editor, Barbara Scott—
you're the best.*

Contents

Introduction

To me, anyone who plays something called an extreme sport must be a little bit nuts. I found, though, that the people in this book are extremely down-to-earth and rooted in the Rock of Jesus Christ, with their eyes securely shining toward heaven. This book was a real pleasure to write because for once, I was able to make direct contact and meet the lively personalities behind these extremely dedicated sports personalities.

Look for them in the news. They'll be there!

1

Greg Albertyn:
Called to Race

Sport	Motocross and Supercross
Personal	Home: South Africa, California Personal interests: Jet-Ski, go-carting, fishing, hanging out Wife: Amy

Motocross Highlights	1992—World 125cc Motocross
	    Champion
	1993—World Motocross Champion, 250cc Class
	1994—World Motocross Champion, 250cc Class
	1999—AMA Motocross Nationals
	    250cc Champion
	Retired: 2000

Contact	Website: http://www.Albee1.com

Heart banging in his chest, his right hand on the throttle, feet balancing his bike, Greg Albertyn gets ready to race motocross.

The 250cc main event begins with another great start by Albertyn, who represents Team Suzuki. His competition, a rider from the Yamaha team, burns up the track beside him, their handlebars smacking and bashing as they whiz around the circle toward the first jump.

As lap one unfolds, Albertyn barely holds the lead over the Yamaha cyclist and a Suzuki teammate. But as the race rages on, Albertyn looks unstoppable, turning in amazing lap times and building on his lead ... until a Team Honda rider blasts through the pack and races up next to Albertyn, forcing him inside and toward the jumps.

Up the ramp, both motocrossers hit the top and fly forty feet through the air. Albertyn lands the jump, pops a wheelie, and heads toward the next one.

Greg Albertyn loves motocross competition—with good reason. He's one of the best racers alive. He has won the world championship three times. But it's not success that causes Greg's heart to race.

"I love motocross because it's one of the most exciting sports in the world," he explains. "The rush of high speeds, the fast and high jumping, guys banging handlebars, the first-turn action—it's definitely the most exciting and adrenaline-filled sport in the world, in my opinion. I feel honored to be able to make a living doing what I love to do."

Extreme Quiz

What is the difference between motocross and supercross?

- Motocross is done on an outdoor natural dirt track. There are high jumps, but the higher speeds are what make it attractive to many racers.
- Supercross is done inside in a stadium. The track is tighter with larger jumps.

Motocross Trivia

During a race, a motocross rider's heart can reach 220 beats per minute—more than three times the normal resting heart rate! And though fans might watch an outdoor race in 70-degree comfort, on the track—and on the bikes—the temperature tops 100 degrees.

Greg grew up in South Africa, playing rugby and basketball. But motorcycle racing hooked him early on. Greg talked his father into buying him a racing bike when he was eight years old. For the next four years, he and his brother entered and won competitions. One day his mom was praying for twelve-year-old Greg's safety, when suddenly she felt a clear impression from God that he wanted Greg to race motorcycles professionally. Greg recalls, "After that prayer, my mom read an article about Verdi Spencer, who was a road-race world champion. She told me about it, and ever since then my goal was to be world champion."

Greg became a professional racer at age seventeen and moved to Europe, where he could race against the greatest names in the sport. Greg says, "That was one of the hardest things I have ever had to do in my life—leave my family and friends in South Africa. Everything I had grown up with, everything I was accustomed to, I had to leave behind. I moved to a different country [Belgium], with different food and culture and language. I was basically alone, although my brother came with me early on, and my family came over for a little while. It was very difficult. That's one of the times when I really drew closer to the Lord and really got to know him—and relied on the Holy Spirit on a day-to-day basis."

Two years later in 1992, Greg won his first 125cc world championship. He was thrilled. Everything he'd ever dreamed of came true as he clinched the title in Japan. "I don't think any win or championship can match up to that," he says. "It was such an incredible sensation about something I had dreamed about since I started racing."

The next year he moved up to the 250cc world championships—the elite class of world motocross racing. Many racers from the 125 and 500 class were moving into 250s, lured by the prestige of the competition. A lot of people told Greg he couldn't win in the 250cc class because he was a 125 rider! Greg proved them wrong. "When it came down to

Motocross Trivia

A typical supercross race lasts about thirty minutes.

the racing," he says, "that was the best overall year of my career for results. I think I won nine out of sixteen Grand Prix events, along with the 250 world championship."

He wanted to come to the U.S. to race, but it didn't work out. So Greg stayed in Europe and worked on repeating his title. He remembers, "In the first four races, I struggled. I was not doing well. I was getting used to my new Suzuki, but I had lost a bit of confidence. Then I told myself, 'You are not going to lose this 250 world championship; you better get your act together and get motivated.' The fifth race of the series, I won, and from then on it

Extreme Quiz

What are the main types of motorcycles used in motocross and supercross?

- Honda
- Suzuki
- Yamaha
- Kawasaki
- KTM

started getting better and better. I won my third championship in a row that year."

Greg was on a roll. But then, while leading at the Motocross des Nations in Switzerland, disaster struck. "I had a totally freak thing happen to me," he recalls. "A deer ran out of the bushes onto the track, and I hit it. That was unbelievable! Then a week later, I broke the navicular bone in my wrist."

It looked like Greg was out for the season, but two months later he was racing again. Then he signed a new contract and came to the U.S. to ride for Team Suzuki. In the U.S., though, things were very different from Europe. "One of the toughest things," he says, "was adapting to the supercross tracks. I definitely underestimated how difficult they were."

But that didn't slow him down: "Being the kind of guy who wants to win at all costs, I would go over there and go over my limit and end up crashing. It's taken me five years to realize that sometimes it's better not to give it 110 percent [too early in the season] but to tone it down to 90 percent to be able to stay healthy until the end of the season."

Racing dirt bikes isn't Greg's only passion, of course. He became a Christian at age eight, and his commitment to the Lord has grown over the years. He says, "My mom led me to the Lord. She asked me if I wanted to pray and ask Jesus into my heart,

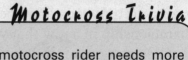

Motocross Trivia

A motocross rider needs more than a bike. Here are a few other items in a rider's arsenal.

- Helmet — This is the most important piece of equipment. It has to fit right to protect a rider's head.
- Goggles — These keep dirt from getting into the eyes.
- Chest protector — Protects against rocks and mud — and softens the blow in an accident.
- Jersey — A long-sleeve shirt. If you have sponsors, you put their logos on your jersey.
- Gloves — These protect against calluses and also keep a rider's hands from getting skinned by flying rocks.
- Pants — Jeans are one option. Some riders wear custom pants emblazoned with sponsors' logos.
- Boots — These keep a rider from breaking an ankle and also absorb impact on turns.

which I did. And about at the same time, I got my first motorcycle. I believe that was God's will for my life. At that time, I started coming home from school wanting to read my children's Bible that my mom had given me. Through my life, and in my career, I've had so many times when I've had opportunities to get so close to the Lord and grow in Him, especially during the difficult times. That's what God sends trials and tests to us for. If everything went perfectly all the time, why would we need God?"

So why did Greg become a Christian?

"Originally, I became a Christian," he says, "because it was something my mom explained to me, and then I made the decision. She told me what Jesus had done for me on the cross, and I thought that was very cool. It wasn't just, 'Hey, I'm going to accept Jesus into my life.' It was a supernatural thing. I could literally feel the presence of God, and there is no question about that. I could feel the Holy Spirit with me, and that became more and more evident as time went on. I look at the things and patterns that have happened in my life, both good and bad, and I give thanks and glory to God for everything that has happened to me. Through God and God alone there is life, and it's life abundant."

In early 1999, Greg married Amy, a young woman he met in California. He says, "The Lord definitely brought her into my life at the right time. We really clicked. We have a special relationship. She's been a real support and blessing."

A blessing indeed: The year Greg got married, he won the motocross 250cc championship, which had eluded him for five years.

Many people have ridden a motorcycle, but Greg says that racing these machines in supercross and motocross is a different world. In fact, it's like experiencing two different races at the same time. He notes, "I'm racing *against* other riders, especially in supercross, when the other riders are very close to me. But I'm also racing the track; I need to be smooth, I need to be precise, and I must make consistent lap times every lap."

Greg says that top riders must maintain a dual concentration: "You can't just think about the track. You can't just ride around thinking 'I'm going to do this obstacle now ... or whatever. Because you throw in the other riders—they are constantly changing their lines. They can block you or pass you. You need to be very aware and look out for other riders coming inside of you, pushing you to the outside, cutting you off here or there. You need to almost have eyes in the back of your head! It's not just a matter of going as fast as you can. You always need to be thinking and planning and using your head."

Many racers endure this demanding competition all year, but Greg likes to take a break occasionally. He takes a full month off. In past years he has gone back to South Africa to see family, do some fishing, and hang out with his wife and friends. He also likes to hit the beach.

Greg's racing success has earned him attention from television and magazines. But he says that what is portrayed in the media doesn't give the full picture of who he is as a person.

He explains, "I think that so many people put sports and entertainment figures on a pedestal. I would like people to know that I'm just a regular guy, an everyday type of person. I do have a God-given talent that I've tried to use to the best of my ability. I believe that everyone has a talent, whether it's business, computers, athletics, or whatever. I don't want people to look up to me and think 'He is this great guy!' I'm just a regular person with all the faults that come with being human. I would like for people to know that I am a down-to-earth normal guy."

Greg will remain a force in motocross racing, as he opens a school to train young racers how to win. He considers it a ministry and something God also has called him to do. "I get all my confidence from the Lord," he says. "So many people base their security in wealth, in their families, in their health, things like that. My Rock is God. I know that if everything were to fall away tomorrow—my family, my wealth, my finances, my racing—I would still have God. And that's what's most important."

Greg says he will encourage young racers to "ride with the Lord. The Bible calls us to be ambassadors

Motocross Testimony

Greg Albertyn

Even when he suffered an injury-plagued period from 1995 to 1998, Greg Albertyn maintained his Christian witness. He says, "I believe God has put me here for a reason and a purpose. Even during those difficult times when I couldn't understand why I was going through them, people would say, 'Greg, we appreciate your witness. Even though you're not winning — even though you're having a tough time — you are still smiling and giving God the glory.'"

On July 31, 2000, Greg announced his retirement, effective at the end of the 2000 season — a season that saw him break his leg during a practice run in Atlanta. He says, "It was a very difficult decision, one of the most difficult decisions I've made in my entire life. Ever since I've been an adult I've been racing professionally. I don't have a lot of expertise in other areas of life, but I'm happy about my decision. I'm sure I will have some emotional ups and downs about it in the near future. But I've felt that if I can't do my job at 100 percent, then it's time to do something else. I've lost that motivation and drive to do it 100 percent.

"I really appreciate all the fans and their support over the years. It's been an incredible career, and I've been extremely blessed. The Lord has now given me an awesome jump start to my future!"

for Christ," he says, "And I hope that's what they're seeing in me. Yes, I make mistakes. Yes, I'm like every other person out there. But God is in me. I want them to see that."

So race on, Greg, and keep training the motocross stars of tomorrow. But most of all, keep on track with the Lord!

Extreme Profile

Natalie and Chris Nelson
Conquering Mountains, Speaking the Truth

They live in the shadow of Mammoth Mountain — 11,053 feet of wonder and snow in the Sierras of California. The ski runs there evoke danger, with names like Hangman's Hollow, Wipe Out, and Paranoid Flats.

Here, sibling snowboarders Natalie and Chris Nelson spend at least two hundred days a year, making moves, doing tricks, jumping mounds, and, in general, tearing up the mountain.

Now twenty-three years old, Natalie knows how dangerous the mountain can be. She has suffered messed-up knees, a broken wrist, a sprained shoulder, and many other problems in her stab at snowboarding greatness.

Her twenty-one-year-old brother, Chris, has also experienced his share of injuries, to say nothing of almost dying in an avalanche. A best friend was "almost sucked under," says Chris. "He thought he was gonna die."

"Snowboarding can be dangerous," says Natalie. "But it's so much fun. I love the rush. I love going as fast as I think I can go, feeling the wind rushing past my face, and then pushing the edge a little more. But at the same time, I play it safe.

"Sometimes you see some people going all out, just reckless, and they get hurt so badly. You're like, 'Why didn't you use a little caution there?'"

Chris is more of a daredevil than Natalie, but he doesn't push the limits too far when he knows there's danger lurking.

"I won't go out and blindly jump off stuff without knowing where I'm gonna land," he says. "But you can't afford to be too conservative, either. To get better at this sport, you've got to be willing to take some risks. But I don't take it too far."

Snowboarding as a lifestyle also has its dangers. But Natalie and Chris, being committed Christians, do not step into the party-hearty, drinking, and drugging ways of many of their competitors.

"There's a stereotype that all snowboarders are into sex and drugs and alcohol," explains Chris. "Everybody's not into that scene, but a lot of 'em are. It's pretty prevalent."

"Oh, man," adds Natalie, "a lot of people like to party. It can get pretty wild."

Chris and Natalie, however, have firmly set limits. "We'll hang out with them and have fun with them all day," says Natalie. "We might still hang with them at night, but we're different. We don't drink, we don't cuss, we don't smoke, and we don't sleep around. We're just not into those things."

They're Christians, Natalie explains, and their faith comes first.

She notes, "People respect us for taking a stand. And a lot of them will ask questions about why we feel that way. They'll say, 'I have to do these things to have fun.' And we'll be like, 'No, you don't.' They'll say, 'Why are you so happy?' And then we can tell them about Jesus.

"It's amazing how much of a testimony you can give just by being yourself."

Chris feels the same way as his sister — and he notes that maintaining high standards isn't always easy. "The hardest times are when you travel somewhere for a competition, and you're kind of on your own," he says. "Sometimes you're pretty much the only Christian in the whole group. So you'll stay in your condo or wherever while everybody else goes out to bars and stuff. They'll come back and say, 'Why didn't you go?' And I'll say, 'I'm a Christian, and I don't really need to go. I have fun doing other stuff.'

"Sometimes that's hard to do, because you want to be with the group but not a part of it. You want to have fun like everyone else, but you don't want to do all the stuff they're doing. You wish they could have fun doing other things, and you want to set that example.

"But saying no is kind of easy compared to explaining *why* you're saying no. They start asking all these hard questions that I don't always have answers to."

Natalie and Chris often invite friends to Bible studies to find out more about the life they live. Some of them have become Christians.

Chris and Natalie are committed to their God — and to their sport. Natalie has her eyes set on the 2002

Olympics. Several years ago, she finished second in the U.S. national championships. But since then, injuries have sidelined her from the big events.

Chris has Olympic dreams as well.

He says, "I'm not good enough to make the [2002] Olympics, but I hope I will be good enough four years from now."

While preparing for the Olympics, Natalie spends a lot of time working with the Mammoth Mountain search-and-rescue team. She never knows what they'll find. It could be someone with a broken leg, or worse.

"Maybe it'll be a dead body," says Natalie, who has found a few. "It can get pretty gross."

Natalie's long-term goal is to become a licensed paramedic. She also has strong interests in diving. Occasionally she is asked to look for people who may have drowned. Once, she discovered the body of a man who had been boiled in a hot spring. "He didn't look human," she says. "I had a hard time dealing with that image for a while.

"But I love doing search and rescue. It's such an adventure, and I love to be able to help people who need help. That's just the way God made me. I was born that way."

2

Jay Haizlip:
From Skateboard Hero to Evangelist

Personal	Height: 5'9" Weight: 155 Birth date: October 28, 1963 Hometown: Atlanta, Georgia Wife: Christy Kids: Newt (18), Baylen (13), and Paris-Ann (16 months)
Personal Interest	skateboarding, hanging out with family, speaking in schools
Awards and Honors	Featured in various magazines (*Thrasher, Skateboarding, TransWorld*) Won numerous skateboarding contests all over the U.S. First team rider for the Visions Company (early 1980s) Appeared in many ads for clothing stores—and in various videos
Contact	Website: *http://www.getagriponline.com*

*T*he first thing you notice is the vert ramp, ten to twelve feet high and resembling a huge U-shaped half-tunnel. In a moment, Jay Haizlip will jump onto the ramp from the top, whip down the side to the transition at the bottom, roar across the floor, and then zip back up the other side to grind his wheels on the edge. Perfect grinder!

Now for the inverted air on the other side. Jay's wheels pound on the ramp with an awesome driving noise he wishes they could reproduce in a rock band. He jets up the other side of the vert, reaches down with his right hand, and grips the skateboard. With his left hand, he grabs the lip of the ramp, leaps, and suddenly he's airborne, upside down, wowing the crowd, turning in midair and coming down with his face to the sky. A front-side inverted air. Hard to do. But not for Jay Haizlip.

Who *is* this guy?

In the 1980s Jay became a household name to families. And he's now been skateboarding for twenty-seven years.

Jay started when he was only ten years old. By the time he was fourteen, he began to ride for several sponsors, such as GNS Skateboards, which was one of the top companies in the world at the time. He says, "I was mainly a vert rider back then, and we were a crazy bunch of guys."

In skateboarding there are two different styles: street style and vert, which means skating on the big ramps, where you can soar high in the air and perform all kinds of impressive tricks. Jay says there aren't many guys who ride vert these days, but back then it was the most popular form of the skateboarding art.

Jay rode for Alva, Visions, Independent Trucks, and other companies in his early days. He says, "I was in their magazines all the time, on the cover of *Thrasher*, and in the anniversary edition in 1988. I'm still featured in several magazines nowadays."

He hasn't lost his skating edge, either, even though he's thirty-seven years old. In February 2001 Jay was featured at "The Gathering of Legends" in California, with many other well-known names in the business.

Jay found out fairly early in his career that the professional skateboarding world could be a dangerous, drug-filled one. As his fame and fortunes mounted, he turned to cocaine and its cousin, crack. At one point in his life, Jay was so whacked

So, You Wanna Buy a Skateboard?

Several companies — including Christian firms such as Renaissance — make skateboards. Jay rides a model made by Madrid. It's important to note that some companies sell boards with vulgar or satanic trappings. One even produces a form in which a person can "sell his soul to Satan" and earn a free T-shirt.

What to look for in a board — besides NO satanic influence?

1. Find the length that's right for your height and the type of skating you like to do. An experienced salesperson can help you find the best board for you. Jay favors a thirty-one-inch board.
2. Width is important. For vert skating, you need to be able to move about and stay comfortably on your board, so you need a wide model.
3. Hardness of wheels. Density determines speed and how the board handles. Jay prefers really hard wheels for maximum speed. If you're a beginning skater and want more control — and you aren't as concerned with speed — you may prefer softer wheels.
4. Concavity. New-style boards feature a pronounced, concave curve. Jay, however, prefers the straighter boards. He says, "You have to find what fits you. It affects the way you do tricks."

out on cocaine that he often took his baby son with him on drug buys. With his son on his hip, he'd fork over the hard-earned dollars that would get him his next high.

Drugs had been a part of Jay's life since childhood. When he was only five years old, his teenage mother left him at a party, where he recalls, "People were getting me drunk. They were blowing pot in my face. They thought it was cute and cool. I remember bouncing off the walls of this hotel and then going out into the parking lot and falling on my face, throwing up, and then my mother coming back. That was the first experience with alcohol and drugs that I remember."

This became normal life for Jay. He went to parties, drank alcohol, and did drugs all the time. By age eleven, he was getting high on marijuana every day.

It was at this time that skateboarding rose in popularity with teens. Jay had a natural flair for it, even though he didn't aspire to become a famous skateboarder. He soon found himself at the top, a pro boardmaster, making lots of money and winning contests and prizes. He used his big-money purses to finance his drug habit. His daring, risky moves on the skateboard expressed what he felt inside—anger, hatred, the desire to hurt himself, and push boundaries.

As Jay rode a wave of celebrity status, his need for drugs escalated.

He says, "Back in the seventies and eighties, skateboarding, drugs, and punk rock music all went together. That was a big part of my life. Eventually, I lost everything that meant anything to me, and drugs became my life."

Jay's life, as you can imagine, was not pretty at that time. He remembers, "I disappeared and faded off the scene in the middle 1980s because of my involvement in drugs. I was in my early twenties. I had gotten married and had a child. I reached a point where I thought of suicide daily; I was constantly depressed, even when I was doing drugs. It was horrible. I placed myself in drug treatment centers, rehab, counseling, twelve-step programs, psychiatrists, and I was even sentenced to prison for six months for possession of drugs. Finally, after trying

Skateboard Trivia

The most awesome skateboarding trick of all time is Tony Hawk's "900." It took ten years to perfect. To perform this one, Tony rolls to the top of a ramp, then sails out above it and performs 2-1/2, 360-degree revolutions while holding onto his board. Then he makes a perfect landing back on the ramp.

everything the world had to offer—and don't get me wrong, I really tried to do what all the programs said to do—it reached a point where I was out partying and on crack for three days and nights in a row. I came home and fell on the edge of my bed and started crying. I called out to God."

It was so bad at that point that Jay says, "I remember when my son was just a little baby in diapers; I had a homemade pipe made out of a can, and I had thrown this rock [crack cocaine] on it. I was sitting there shaking, trying to do this hit, and my son comes around and he's standing there looking up at me. I'm shaking, taking this hit, and at the same time I'm feeling so guilty because my baby's sitting there watching me. I was so tormented. My life was just being ripped apart."

God was after Jay, though, and it seemed that as things went from bad to worse, he found a Lord who cared.

One night at home, he snorted cocaine and ended up having a terrible reaction to it. "I started freaking out," he says. "I had all this cocaine, and I thought somebody was at my back door—and somebody was at my front door. I don't know who I thought it was, but I just thought people were trying to get in to get me. I ran to a tree, and nobody was there. Then I ran around my house. It was like a voice was saying, 'Oh, they're running around your house.' I had already determined that I was going to take a butcher knife and was going to ram it into whomever was there."

Jay was so zonked on the drugs that night that he might have done something truly violent. He says, "The scary thing is that if one of my neighbors had been out walking a dog or something like that, an innocent person just out there for whatever reason at six in the morning, I would have killed them, because I'd snapped."

Somehow Jay made it back into the house and crumpled on the edge of his bed. He burst into tears, filled with despair. He didn't want to live; his life was awful, and he wanted to be free from his drug dependency. He finally looked up at the ceiling and cried, "God, if you're real, why won't you help me? Because you know I don't want to be like this."

God heard the cry for help. At the time, Jay was an automobile salesman. One night he had to pick up a car that had problems. The car's owner told Jay how God had changed everything for him, that he'd been an alcoholic, frequently wrecking cars while drunk. Then one day his thirteen-year-old son told him about Jesus, and he was converted.

Jay couldn't get the man's testimony out of his mind, and when he returned the repaired car to its owner, he stayed at the man's house for pizza. The

Skateboarding Tricks Perfected by Jay

Ollies — making the board pop up by just using his feet.

Inverted Air — Rolling up the edge of a ramp, Jay grabs his board with one hand and flips upside-down. With the other hand, he grips the lip of the ramp and does a one-handed handstand — before returning his board to the ramp.

Edger — going up the ramp to the edge — with the wheels only millimeters from the rim of the ramp — then turning around without going beyond the ramp.

Grinder — going up on the edge of the ramp, turning, then grinding the board's underside along the top of the ramp. A skater can also grind down a stair railing.

Super High Frontside and Backside Airs — blasting beyond the top of the ramp and soaring very high. Frontside is one direction; backside is the other direction. Frontside means facing the sky; backside means facing the ramp.

man talked more about Jesus. Jay was riveted. He recalls, "It really was blowing me away. He was acting like Jesus was his best friend, like Jesus was right there with us. I was almost looking around the room because I thought, 'Where is this guy? You're acting like he's right here.'"

Jay finally asked the man how to get saved. He didn't even know what saved meant. But he decided that he would get saved—then go down the street and find some cocaine. At least, in his mind, the issue would be settled.

Advice from the Top—Jay Haizlip's Advice for Young Skaters

Skateboarding takes a lot of practice. You have to keep doing it; don't give up. You don't become the best overnight. A lot of times you'll go to a place where kids are skating and you'll get intimidated because they're so much better than you are. But in the end, skateboarding is about having fun. So have fun and a good time at it. You'll get better with practice."

But that wasn't the end of it. The man showed Jay several verses in the Bible, including Romans 10:9–10, which tell of believing in Jesus and publicly proclaiming that faith. Jay didn't hesitate. He knew God was speaking. "It was like all of heaven was there convicting me," he says. So the man helped Jay repeat a prayer of trust in Christ.

As the man sensed that other things were wrong in Jay's life, including witchcraft, he prayed to break the power of the devil too. God answered those prayers. Jay was set free.

Jay recalls, "I didn't have any wild, demonic manifestations or anything like that, but I just felt all the hurt leaving, all the pain leaving, all that junk. And then as we were kneeling there praying, the man asked God to fill me with the Holy Spirit. I didn't even know who Jesus was, much less the Holy Spirit, and then all of a sudden Jesus just baptized me in the Holy Spirit while I was sitting there. Man, I knew that I was changed. When I stood up I told him, 'Whoa, man, something's happened to me.'"

He left the house feeling high all over, but it was not the drug high he was used to; it was better, a high from God. He says, "It was real, it was pure, and it was from heaven. I threw my hands up, and I just started screaming, 'I'm saved! I'm saved! I'm saved!' I felt so good."

That was Jay Haizlip's turnaround. He now works with youth, telling them that Christ can break any evil power in their lives and set them free. He speaks all over the U.S. in public high school assembly programs where he gives his "Get a Grip with Jay Haizlip" talks and rallies.

He says that kids today "have pain from abandonment. They have pain from abuse, neglect, or bad things that have happened to them. When they drink alcohol or get involved in drugs, it medicates that hurt. I try to prevent them from going down the same road that I went down, because, unfortunately, most people that go down the road don't make it back. I want to see people saved. I want to see people change. I want to see kids that have been delivered from drugs—and pursuing God with their whole heart."

If you attend one of Jay's rallies, you'll hear him say, "Above all, make the right choices. Just one bad choice can mess you up for the rest of your life."

The choices we make, whether they're in our normal daily living or in our extreme sports, is who we really are. Jay says, "Who we ultimately become in life depends on the choices we make. We're not born losers; we're born choosers. What we do is our choice, and we can't blame it on anyone else. We all have to answer for what we've done. Don't make a bad choice that will affect your entire future.

"And dream big dreams. Go after them. You can do anything you want. A scripture I use is, 'This day I have set before you life or death, blessing or cursing.' That's where each of us is every day."

Today Jay speaks to as many as twenty-five thousand young people a week in his Get a Grip program. Because he speaks in many public schools, he doesn't specifically mention Jesus or God in the Get a Grip talks. But he uses these talks to invite kids to evangelistic rallies later in the week. At these events, he is free to discuss faith in God. Jay says, "We have as many as two to five thousand teenagers who come [to the evangelistic events], and I share the gospel."

Jay proclaims God's saving power with his whole heart. Though his skateboarding competition days are over, his life with Jesus is still only beginning.

3

Katie Brown: Climbing Sheer Walls for Christ

Sport	Climbing, Difficulty Climbing
Personal	Home: Rock Springs, Georgia Height: 5'1" Weight: 95 Birth date: November 30, 1980
Climbing Highlights	1998—AFCF National Champion, Difficulty Climb 1999—World Cup Champion ESPN X-Games Gold Medalist (four times)

Photo by: Jorge Visser

sheer wall in front of you. Sixty to a hundred feet straight up. "You're going to climb that?" people often ask Katie Brown. She just shrugs and goes to it.

On this day, with nothing but her fingers and toes holding on, Katie hung forty feet above the ground. She pressed into the wall, stabilizing herself, but peered at the wall above her, searching for a handhold.

Just fifteen years old, Katie was scaling a wall in what is called difficulty sport climbing. The X Games, held that year in Rhode Island, charted a course for contestants to climb walls and prove their mettle against time, heat, and endurance.

Katie started the competition early, but the fifteen women before her had all made mistakes in judgment and fallen, protected by the safety line that keeps them from hurting themselves. Katie had less than a yard to go to be the first one to climb all the way. If she did it, she'd win.

Tiny knobs, cuts, and divots in the wall created handholds. Confidently, Katie reached up six inches and grabbed the next knot-like knob. Then with a hard push, she swung herself up another foot.

Off (and On) the Wall with Katie Brown

C ompetition walls range from thirty to a hundred feet in height. They can be very tall, particularly in Europe. Competitions usually take place inside, but sometimes they are held outdoors on walls of sandstone, limestone, or conglomerate rock.

Competition rock and wall climbing is one of the most arduous sports in the world. It takes tremendous strength for competitors to haul their bodies up a rock or manufactured wall face. It also requires agility, concentration, and guts.

Katie has them all, and more.

When she climbs, she explains, she's not up there alone on the wall. "For me," she says, "climbing involves a lot of prayer, because I don't have the strength to do it on my own."

At five-foot-one and only ninety-five pounds, Katie doesn't look like a superhero, although she climbs like Spiderwoman. She has won several national and international events. She says, "Climbing is so challenging, mentally and physically. I marvel at how people can climb without having somebody bigger to rely on."

Just one more foot to go! So with one more grab, locking on with her fingers, Katie had it. She whisked over the edge of the wall to finish. Hundreds of people below cheered! Katie was the youngest competitor in the whole group to win. More than a champion, she had courage, discipline, and determination all wrapped into her small, agile body.

Katie started climbing at age twelve, when she moved to Lexington, Kentucky, from Denver, Colorado. She began attending sessions at Climb Time, a climbing gym in town. The instructors saw she had talent and advised her to enter competitions. She tried several junior competitions, and then in 1995 she took the junior national title in her age group. Later that year, she grabbed another title at the World Junior Championships in Laval, France. It's been up, up, and away since then. She has won several of the most difficult competitions, including the World Cup, the X Games Difficulty Climb (three times), and the prestigious ARCO Invitational.

Another highlight in Katie's climbing career came in April 1999—when she on-sighted (see "Climbing Terms" for a definition) Omaha Beach, an often-climbed but extremely difficult route in Kentucky's Red River Gorge. One day, her third consecutive day spent climbing several difficult routes, Bill Ramsey—a climber who had done the

Climbing Terms

- **Bouldering**—Usually performed on low-lying rocks about ten to sixteen feet high. This form of climbing involves no ropes or protective gear. So climbers don't attempt to go so high that they would be seriously injured if they fell.

- **Redpoint**—Repeatedly practicing the moves of a climb until it can be done without error.

- **On-Sight Climbing**—Scaling a rock with no prior knowledge of the features and difficulties of the climb.

- **Flash**—Like on-sight climbing, except the climber has prior knowledge of the rock and the moves needed to scale it.

- **Difficulty Climbing**—the category of sport climbing in which the winner is the climber who reaches the highest point of a wall (usually forty-five to sixty feet high) without falling. These competitions are usually held on manufactured walls. Each climber wears a harness with a safety rope attached, preventing falls all the way to the ground. The rope is held by a spotter on the ground. On the climbing route are a series of numbered clips. Each climber has to clip in at each number. And competitors are not allowed to study the route ahead of time.

- **Dyno**—Short for "dynamic motion," a momentum move or a small jump that a climber makes to reach hand- or footholds that are out of normal reach.

first complete ascent of The Gorge—told Katie to try it. But he made no mention of how difficult it was. Katie didn't hesitate but donned the gear and started to climb.

"I just thought," she recalls, "well, since I'm tired, I might as well just try it and see how I go. I just started climbing it, and the higher I got, the less I wanted to fall—and the more I wanted to do it [complete the climb]. So I just got more and more determination as I went."

The route Katie was following features a signature move at a point called Omaha Beach. "It's such a struggle to get off [Omaha Beach]," Katie says. "It's like a big shelf that you have to climb over."

Katie spent some time figuring out how to clear the Beach. To achieve her goal, she did a great move called a dyno. That was quite unlike her usual smooth, direct style. Finishing up, she learned she had achieved something that no other woman has done in climbing history: she made an on-sight ascent of a 5.13d-level climb (one of the highest difficulty levels in climbing.) The only others to have on-sighted this climb are two men, Switzerland's Elie Chevieux and Australia's Garth Miller.

Katie says her love for climbing—and her approach to the sport—remind her of a favorite Scripture she found in the Psalms: "I lift up my eyes to the hills—where does my help come from? My help comes from the LORD, the Maker of heaven and earth. He will not let your foot slip—he who watches over you will not slumber" (Psalm 121:1–3).

She notes, "I know that I couldn't have done what I've done without being a Christian. It takes away a lot of the pressure, because you know that God's not going to condemn you if you don't win. So there's nothing to worry about."

Katie finds it difficult to understand people who climb but have no faith or confidence in God. "When I see others competing," she says, "I wonder how I could compete if I didn't have faith in God. It boggles me how people can get up there and climb with nothing to lean on beside themselves."

Katie became a Christian at age eight at a camp where the speaker encouraged the kids to pray to receive Christ. Katie listened and spoke the prayer and became a Christian that night. Life as a believer hasn't always been easy, though. In fact, she says sometimes it's harder to be a Christian than not. But, she asserts, she will always climb for the Lord, not herself.

Katie's focus on God helps her handle setbacks. At an ARCO Rock Masters event in Italy, for example, it looked like Katie would clinch the championship. She savored the thought of collecting the eight-thousand-dollar prize.

"Everybody was congratulating me," she recalls. "Then the judges came up to me and said I was disqualified."

The judges claimed Katie had stepped on a bolt during her climb, an illegal move. It supposedly gave her an advantage over other climbers. They had even watched a videotape of Katie's climb to make sure their decision was correct.

"I didn't feel I had stepped on the bolt, but sometimes your foot bumps it by accident," says Katie. "But I didn't want to argue about it. I just said, 'Okay, that's fine.' And then I went off and cried by myself and I came to the conclusion that I must have been thinking too much about winning the money, which shouldn't be important anyway."

Katie realizes that someday she won't be able to climb as easily as she does now. And that's why her life doesn't center only on her sport. "I love climbing," she says. "It's a very individualistic sport, where you pretty much have the freedom and independence to do things your own way. And I love being outdoors.

"But there are a lot of other things I want to do. I want to do some Bible translation work. I might like to be a missionary at some point. I just know that I want to do things other than climbing the rest of my life."

When she looks back on her career someday, one particular competition will probably rank as the high point: "Without question," she says, "the first X Games I ever did [in 1996]. I won in difficulty climbing." She was a wild-card climber, and that was part of the thrill.

"I didn't have the ranking to get invited [to the competition], but they always invite an extra person, just because. To me, I just went for fun. I didn't have any expectations of myself. Nobody else had any expectations of me. It was a lot more fun for that reason. After you win so many times, you're expected to win, and you expect yourself to win. There are a lot more hang-ups. There are many

Climbing Pointers

- Always keep three points (two hands and a foot or two feet and a hand) on the wall or the rock. Fingers and toes can slip from their holds. Be sure three points are secure before you reach for a hold with your free hand or foot.
- Save your energy. Climbers know that their arms will get tired first. Learn to move quickly when using your arms and rest when more weight is on your feet.
- Spend time on the rock. The best way to build strength and get better at climbing is to climb as much as you can.

more mental games you have to play. In that competition, it was just a lot more enjoyable."

By the way, Katie was only fifteen when she won the event.

Now twenty-one, Katie has many good climbing years ahead of her. But who knows—maybe she'll go to Tibet, translate a Bible, and climb Mt. Everest while she's at it. Now wouldn't that be amazing!

Katie has some advice for the young climbers of tomorrow.

"First of all, I encourage them to definitely get out there and try rock climbing," she says. "Young people are naturals at it. It's a clean thrill, totally safe, and a great confidence builder. Also, as you get older, life is bound to get more complicated and more confusing. So I think it's important to always try and remember that Christ's love will carry you through whatever happens, even if today it feels impossible to make it to tomorrow."

Katie has proven herself already to be one amazing lady. We'll be looking for her on a high wall, or mountainside, sometime soon. Although, don't expect her to be there for long. She likes to get to the top. She never spends a lot of time just hanging around.

Sometimes the Climbing Is the Easy Part

KATIE BROWN'S FAVORITE CLIMBING STORY

I will never forget the first time I went to Europe for a competition. It seemed like every time everything went wrong *before* the competition, things would go great *in* the competition. The opposite was also true. If things went smoothly before the competition, then something would usually go wrong later. I have come to the conclusion that this was because when everything was going wrong, I was forced to put my trust fully in God. When things went smoothly, I had a tendency to feel like I could do it on my own, and I would forget that it was God's strength, not my own, that allowed me to do well.

Anyway, here's the story: We left from Atlanta and were supposed to fly to New York City and then on to Milan, Italy. On the way to New York, however, the windshield of our airplane shattered, and we had to make an emergency landing in Pittsburgh. (I went up and looked at the windshield after landing — it was like a spiderweb.) We couldn't get out again that night, so everybody from the plane had to stay the night in Pittsburgh.

Just as an aside, during this time I was completely strict with my training schedule. We had it planned that I would miss only two days of climbing on the way to

Italy, but as it turned out I missed three extra days—five days total. I never took more than two days off and was convinced that if I did I would be out of shape. So needless to say, during this whole trip I was practically frothing at the mouth, completely paranoid about being out of shape by the time we got to the competition. (Which, of course, was completely ridiculous and couldn't have been further from the truth.)

Anyway, the next day, after a night of worrying on my part, we flew to New York, only to find that because of our flight's delay, all kinds of planes were overbooked. My mother, being so gracious, decided to give up our seats to someone else. I was extremely upset at the idea of being even later, but as it turned out the next flight was only two hours later, and we got to fly first class (which is heaven).

So, we made our way from the airport to the train station. If you've never been in a train station in Europe, it is very confusing, compounded by the fact that everything is in a foreign language. We had no idea where to go, and didn't know a word of Italian. Finally, this old Italian man came up to us and started pointing and gesturing. He didn't speak any English, but somehow we got the message that if we bought him a cup of coffee he would show us where our train was.

We had no idea, though, if he was taking us to the right train. Also, we thought we had done a smart thing by bringing two big bags instead of four small bags for the two of us. In Europe, that is a bad idea, let me tell you. Our bags would hardly fit on the train. We finally had to stuff them in the aisle and sit on them. When we got to our destination, it was dark, and the train station was deserted. There were some people who had planned on picking us up, but we were two days late at this point.

We spent two hours trying to figure out the phones, even with the help of three Italian people. When we finally called the people who were supposed to pick us up, they said that they couldn't come because it was too late.

Tired and jetlagged, we ended up sleeping in the train station. The next day we got picked up, but European cars are tiny, and our bags would hardly fit in the car, making our driver and his wife quite upset. They drove us to the village where we would be staying and dropped us off at the outskirts. We hefted our gigantic bags, hiked the rest of the way into town, and stopped at the first hotel we saw. We were supposed to have reservations at a different hotel, but at that point we were too tired to care. Needless to say, it was quite an adventure, but it turned out wonderfully. We found our hotel and rented bicycles. The cliffs were very close to the village, so we rode our bikes everywhere.

Extreme Profile

Noah Snyder
A Surfer Catching Waves for Jesus

Noah Snyder never thought much about the ark or the original Noah, but that Old Testament story was destined to change his life. He loved surfing from the moment he caught his first wave at the age of thirteen. A feeling like nothing he'd even known before surged through him, and he knew this was something he wanted to do as long as he lived.

Young Noah began surfing competitively, and by age fifteen, he was beating some of the best in the sport in open competitions. At twenty-one, he decided to become a professional surfer.

Today he surfs all over the world. He still wants to win a major competition; he's finished in the top ten enough times to know he can do it. He loves the big waves.

But his life has had its share of wipeouts. He explains, "There was a lot of pressure because I was popular, so when I would go out surfing, I would always feel like I had to do well — not just for myself but for the people that looked up to me. And I felt I had to portray a certain image."

Part of that image included the temptation to become a big-time partier. That was always in front of him, and although he resisted it, he knew something was out of place in his life.

He recalls, "I was spending time in Florida. I was down there for some contests, and I had some time to think to myself. I had a feeling of emptiness that was brewing inside me. I didn't understand it. I couldn't figure out why I was feeling this way. But I felt the urge to go home."

At home, on the Outer Banks of North Carolina, Noah ran into an old friend who invited him to church.

"It was a time when my mind wasn't on God," he says. "I wasn't thinking about the Lord or thinking about living for the Lord or even becoming a Christian — or any of those things that a lot of people face now when they go to church. It was almost like my mind was pretty clear, but it wasn't on God.

"Rich Workerson was the guest speaker that morning. And when he spoke, it almost felt like he was inside of my body and feeling the hurt that I felt. It was almost like he had experienced my whole life for the past month."

Noah knew something was happening in his heart, and he wanted to go forward to receive Christ, but he was afraid. Three other friends were with him, and he didn't want to embarrass them or be embarrassed by going forward.

However, one of those friends saw Noah raise his hand before the altar call. He asked if Noah had just been saved, and Noah didn't know how to answer him. Then he led Noah gently down to the altar. There, Noah says, "I cried and I wept, but at the same time, I felt a true love in my life that I had never, ever felt before."

In time, his other friends came to the altar too.

The four of them went back to surfing with new faith and a new commitment to spread the Word. Over time, ten other surfers became Christians. Noah feels real strength from his home church and the prayers they send to heaven on his behalf.

"My whole church says they will be praying for me," he says, "praying for this and praying for that. I thank God for allowing me to go to a church like that."

The coolest part about it, though, was where Noah was saved. The church is called The Ark. When Noah accepted Christ at the altar that day, his friend Andy stood up in front of the whole church and told them, "Today we have a professional surfer that got saved in The Ark, and guess what? His name is Noah."

Noah says of that moment, "I just stopped. I thought that was so ironic just how it happened. I mean, everybody says that God has a sense of humor. That's proof of it right there."

Rob Struharik: Wakeboarder Who Will Wow You!

Personal	Birth date: May 11, 1981 Height: 5'6" Weight: 150

Contact	World Wakeboarding
	    Championship Results
	1998—Champion
	1999—3rd
	2000—4th
	The place: Orlando, Florida.
	The event: the 1998 Wakeboarding
	    World Championships.

Rob Struharik, seventeen, is competing. He doesn't expect to take the prize. He just wants to do his best.

The boat speeds up to more than 50 mph, sending out a sharp-tipped wake, perfect to go airborne on. Rob readies himself, his legs limber, his board smooth and in control. The boat gives him a jolt, and he darts toward the wake. Whoa!

He turns on the wake. A Surface 360! Perfectly executed. But that's easy.

For the next 360, he leaves the surface of the water. He's in the air. Twisting. Turning full circle. A 360-degree turn. An Air 360. More difficult. But much more fun too.

Rob slaps down into the water on the other side of the wake, nods to the clapping crowd, and prepares himself for the other tricks of the afternoon, during which he hopes to win his first championship.

And then, he does!

Rob remembers the day well. "There was all this talk and television coverage," he says. "I was just hoping to make the finals. I was still a young pro. I'd never won a tournament at that point, although I'd placed third once. I went out and rode my best. My dad was there. And it turned out that I was the best in the tournament. I got a lot of respect. It was incredible."

That year he won the overall title and got a year-end bonus from his sponsor, Connelly Wake Boards (CWB—it's written all over Rob's wakeboards). Rob says, "All my family was there, and it was a great experience, especially to win the overall title. It's the biggest title in our sport."

As a kid, Rob didn't seem like a title winner. In school, he felt for a long time that he didn't have a place. He was different. He was small. He hadn't found a school sport that suited him.

Then he became a wakeboarder. And things got worse.

"Everybody in high school basically hated me because I was doing something different," he explains. "It was a tough spot to be in.

"But then, they saw me on ESPN for the first time. I was cool from that point on."

He realized that the hypocrisy of public opinion reached even the school level. "It was so double-sided," he says. "Kids can be so mean or so nice. They can either tear you down or build you up, and they usually don't do anything in between."

At seventeen, Rob won his first tournament in Altamonte Springs, Florida. It was billed as the "richest wakeboarding event ever" at the time. Since then, he's managed to finish in the top five the last few years, taking the championship in 1998 and placing high in 1999 and 2000.

So what exactly is this sport that Rob Struharik is so in love with—the sport he's excelled in?

In wakeboarding, a speedboat tows you and you surf on the wakes the boat creates. Your board is smaller than a surfboard; bindings and straps bind you to it. But it's nothing like waterskiing.

The key is to use the boat's wake to go airborne and, while out there in space, perform tricks. In tournaments, the degree of difficulty and skill used in performing tricks is what makes a winner. Each wakeboarder gets two runs—up and back, up and back—performing tricks all the way. At the end, competitors face a double-up, as the boat circles to make a crazy web of waves that can shoot a wakeboarder even higher into the air.

Rob likes the simplicity of his sport and the honesty he can bring to it. "Our generation is just so used to adults being dishonest with us," he says, "that it's easy to lie to other kids. We've been doing it since we were five years old. So whatever I do, I try to be as blunt as possible."

That honesty comes from Rob's background, growing up in a Christian home. He says, "My par-

A rider goes over a jump during the AMA Motocross National at the Glen Helen Raceway in San Bernardino, California.

Photo by: Jon Ferrey / Allsport

Snow boarding in Colorado.

Photo by: Nathan Bilow / Allsport

A rider pulls a trick during the bike stunt competition at the 2001 X-Games at First Union Center in Philadelphia, Pennsylvania.

Photo by: Ezra Shaw / Allsport

Jay Haizlip speaks in public schools, churches, and recently leads one of the fastest growing youth churches in America.

Photo by: JayHaizlip / Get a Grip

Katie Brown climbing Aromas de Mont Groni in Mont Groni, Spain.

Rob Struharik is reaching for a Moby Dick at the 2001 X-Games in Philadelphia, Pennsylvania. This technical move is a flip with a 360-degree spin.

Photo by: Mike Isler / islerphoto

Australian Glyndyn Ringrose relaxing at the 2000 Gotcha Tahiti Pro.

Photo by: Pierre Tostee / tostee.com

Australian Glyndyn Ringrose in action at the 2000 Gotcha Tahiti Pro.

Photo by: Pierre Tostee / tostee.com

Rider Tom Kipp rounding turn 11 at the 1995 World Superbike (WSB) race at Laguna Seca Raceway in Monterey, California.

Photo by: Steve Allen / Frogman Foto

ents were great role models. I was probably thirteen or fourteen before I started appreciating my parents and Christianity. I began to understand what the Lord did for me. It wasn't until I actually understood it that it had any impact in my life. Before that, I was not walking the walk."

But God was there, and he decided to introduce Rob to a new verse: "When I was thirteen, I read Matthew 10:32–33, about publicly acknowledging Christ before others," he says. "Jesus said in that passage that if we confess him before men, he will confess us before his Father and his angels in heaven. And if we deny him before men, he will deny us before his Father. I didn't want that to happen to me. That told me that I was going to have to be bold for Christ. I wanted to serve him wherever I was."

It was a hard thing to learn to do. For a long time he kept relatively quiet about his faith.

"If someone asked me about the Lord," he explains, "I'd tell them I was a Christian. But I wouldn't go out of my way to be bold for the Lord. That has all changed, as I've read verses like that one in Matthew 10. Now I try to bring Jesus Christ into the conversation. I got onto the pro tour at about age fifteen. That summer, being a Christian played a huge part in my life. I wanted to be bold, and I wanted to approach people. So I began to speak up, to actually go up and talk to people."

Ask Rob what the gospel is all about, and this is what he'll tell you:

"It comes down to Romans 10:9, where it says that if you confess with your mouth Jesus as Lord and believe in your heart that God raised him from the dead, you will be saved. That was basically the whole Bible to me—confessing the Lord—and I get really excited about it because I can use that to help people understand Christianity and the truth. I use it when I bring up the subject of the Lord to other people."

Rob enjoys his sport. He likes the speed, the tricks, and the creativity. But most of all, he likes it that he's a Christian in a sport where there aren't many Christians.

"When I went into wakeboarding," he says, "I said that if people like me, they're going to like me as a Christian. They're not going to like me just because I'm cool. As I got a little bit more fame inside the industry, people began to notice stickers on my board or a WWJD bracelet, and they would talk to me about it. Non-Christians would ask, 'What does that sticker mean?' It would turn into a half-hour conversation."

For a while, Rob really got into making those stickers. He says, "When I was seventeen, we made fish stickers to give to people. We also made stickers of Romans 10:9 and Romans 1:16–17—which talks about being bold for Christ—to put on boards and things. I would pass out the stickers. It generated a lot of questions. About that time, the WWJD bracelet came out, so that opened up a lot of conversations too."

Wakeboarder Testimony

Gerry Nunn

Without Jesus in my life, I would be living without any purpose. I know that my career as a wakeboarder is a blessing, and I aim at keeping Jesus first in my life. I am thankful for the Bible (Basic Instructions Before Leaving Earth) and its promises. My favorite verse is Jeremiah 29:11: 'For I know the plans I have for you,' declares the LORD, 'plans to prosper you and not to harm you, plans to give you hope and a future.' "

"Before the tournaments on Sunday mornings, about eight of us would have a little prayer service in our trailer. It was like a chapel service. We didn't think anyone would show up. But the first week we had twenty-five people. Then thirty. Soon we had eighty people at our chapels. We've been having those chapel services at every tournament since.

"It's been great because you see a lot of people change their lives. This year we have a booklet called 'Making the Cut.' And we pass that out. It has personal stories in it."

Rob has had an amazing effect on his sport. In addition to distributing stickers, he and several others began a prayer group that is now a chapel service that meets on Sunday mornings before tournaments.

Often people ask Rob questions about his faith, and he pulls no punches when he answers. Or should we say ... he doesn't try any tricks.

"It's awesome," said Robert Stauffer, Fellowship of Christian Athletes (FCA) area director in Youngstown, Ohio, near Rob's home in Boardman. "It takes a lot for a kid this age to be able to take those kinds of stands, but if I had to pick anybody in the country who would do it, it would be Robert. He's just a solid kid.

"He's very humble. You could probably talk to him for three days and not have any idea what he has accomplished. He's been forced to grow up quickly, because all of the people he competes against are much older. He is spiritually probably one of the most mature kids I have ever met for his age."

Rob appreciates the challenges of being a young Christian in an extreme sport. He says, "I know that I can do a thousand things that are good for people and good for my sport. But then I can swear once in front of people and that's what they'll remember. For people to take my faith seriously and me seriously, I have to be consistent about it. When I do fall, I can't ignore it, though. I need to ask forgiveness.

"I guess some people are watching to see if you'll fall. I know I stumble and fall, but the Lord picks me back up. God's grace has to overcome all the mistakes. People think you need to be perfect to be a Christian, and I tell them you don't. God's grace is what you need, not perfection."

Rob knows how fame and fortune can be a trick. You have to guard against making mistakes and doing things wrong.

"With the Internet now, if somebody even hears something, everyone in the industry knows about it at the click of a button," he says. "You've got to

Wakeboarder Testimony

Emily Copeland

Being a Christian has helped me keep everything in perspective. I have a bigger purpose here on earth than to ride a wakeboard. As an athlete, I just want to be the best at what I do, and as a Christian, I want to be a good role model and let God shine through me. I want others to know they have someone (God) to turn to no matter where they are in their lives or what they have done."

Rob Struharik on "The Perfect Run"

For me, the perfect run always takes place during practice. It usually happens as the sun's setting, there's no wind, and the lake's like a mirror — you can see yourself and the boat, and the red reflection from the sunset. You forget about who's watching you and what muscles are hurting, and you just get in a zone, focusing on the wake of the boat. It's an incredible feeling. It's not about what tricks you're doing or how big you're going; it's about how much you're enjoying it out there, and how good you feel inside, being at one with nature."

watch what you say. It's definitely hard to live up to [Christianity's high standards], and it's definitely uncomfortable at times, knowing that you have that responsibility on you at such a young age. It's so easy to lose your temper.

"The other day I fell, and I just smacked the water with my hand. It wasn't in a real ticked-off mode, but even then I thought that I shouldn't have done that because I don't want people to take that as losing my temper. You just have to watch yourself so much more."

Rob credits his dad as his greatest influence: "He drives the boat in practice. He's never pushy; he never pushed wakeboarding on me. He's pretty laid-back. He made me realize that there are many more things in life that are way more important than your sport. Your mind, for example. The Lord. Your walk with Him. He goes to many of my tournaments. In a lot of ways, he's like a buddy. He hangs with the guys and spends time with us."

Wakeboarder Testimony

Shaun Murray

Shaun asked Jesus into his heart when he was a young child, but as he recalls, it wasn't until he was in high school that he realized the importance of his decision. "I realized that Jesus was a real man that walked this earth and gave His life for me," Shaun says. "I broke down in tears because it meant so much to me, and I didn't know if I could have done the same."

Shaun has tried making his own way in life—and found it didn't work. "I have tried living on my own," he admits, "without God at my side helping me with decisions. Not only does it not work, it just feels empty. It is like I am going about my everyday routine for no reason."

Wakeboarder Testimony

Jesus helps Shaun, one of the world's best at his sport, keep his career in perspective. "I have been able to keep in focus that riding is just riding and nothing more," he says. "Of course, I have days when I get frustrated, but when that happens, I step off my board, get into the boat, and laugh at myself for getting mad. I remember all of the other things I can enjoy in life, like my friends and especially my family. When I begin to feel overwhelmed with responsibilities, I just remember that everything will pass and work out for the best."

What would Shaun like to say to readers of his story?

"One thing that I've learned lately is that you want to strive to be a good Christian, but nobody's perfect. You're not going to be perfect, no matter how hard you try. You have to just accept God's grace and ask Him for forgiveness. That's the only way you can survive, just keep accepting His grace."

He continues, "Start being bold for Jesus when you're young, and it'll be a lot easier when you're older. When I got to the higher years in high school, I had a little more authority and could talk more about my beliefs. But the longer you wait, the harder it is."

Amateur Tournaments

BY ROB SCHOEDEL

*N*ailing your S-Bend? Ready to show off your Bel-Air? Not quite? No problem! Amateur tournament events are your ticket to learning new tricks, watching others rip it up, and testing out your skills as well.

The learning part comes from clinics that are often part of tournaments. Many tournaments reserve a day or two before the competition for clinics led by advanced or pro riders. Generally, a boatload of boarders go out with an instructor, and each takes turns riding. The pro will offer tips throughout each set, so you're nearly guaranteed to make progress.

Contrasted with the clinic, the tournament is a much different event. While the exact structure will vary from contest to contest, the most popular formats are freestyle and expression session.

A freestyle competition is the more structured contest of the two; it's based on an objective rating system. Each trick is worth a predetermined number of points, and each contestant declares which tricks he or she will perform before competing by filling out an attack sheet. There are often penalties for falling, so riders usually choose tricks they feel comfortable with.

Based upon the tricks chosen, riders will be classified in categories such as beginner, intermediate, advanced, and open. It is also common to have additional categories based on age — such as the junior or masters divisions. The tricks can be sophisticated inverted rotating moves (worth more than a thousand points) or as simple as waving to the judge (worth fifty points). . . .

By contrast, contests following the expression session format are much less regimented. The judging is subjective, and point values are awarded based upon three factors:

1. Composition: the variety of tricks you perform
2. Style: making the tricks look smooth, not mechanical — by adding your creative touches to the trick
3. Intensity: how big you go and how hard you try

Rather than precomposing your run, expression sessions allow you to go out and ride, as if you were going out with friends for a short set. Riders are given a specific amount of time, usually two to four minutes to ride. There is no penalty for falling, but the clock doesn't stop, whether you're rippin' it up or sitting in the water.

If you're not feeling like you want to compete, drop by and be a spectator. Tournaments are sponsored events, so you'll often find display booths, food, music, and whatever else can make a great weekend at the lake!

If you do compete, consider using some of these relatively easy tricks:

- Description: Stand on the board for five seconds
- Category: Beginner
- Point Value: 20

Tip on performing this trick: This is a great trick for beginners who are just learning to balance themselves on the board. Helpful hints — keep your arms straight (or slightly bent) but not all the way in to your chest. Spread your hands wide on the handle, with both palms down. Keep your knees bent like shock absorbers to ride out any waves. Focus on twisting your hips so that your upper body is facing the boat and your lower body is keeping the board pointed in the direction of the pull.

- Description: Ride one handed for five seconds
- Category: Beginner
- Point Value: 40

Tip on performing this trick: Now that you're getting more confident, take a hand off the handle and wave to the boat or to those watching from the shore. It doesn't matter which hand you wave with, but make sure you are smiling!

- Description: Cross one wake
- Category: Beginner
- Point Value: 50

Tip on performing this trick: After you've become used to your board, you will want to cross the wakes. The key here is how you position your hips. Focus on twisting your hips so that your upper body is facing the boat and your lower body is keeping the board pointed in the direction of the pull. In order to turn the board to head in either direction, it's just a matter of moving your hips in the direction in which you want to cross the wake. For example, turn your hips to the left and your body positions the board to turn left. Same thing when you turn your hips to the right.

- Description: Cross both wakes
- Category: Beginner
- Point Value: 60

Tip on performing this trick: Crossing one wake or two, it's all the same. Use your hips! In order to turn the board to cross in either direction, move your hips in the direction you want to go. Rotate the hips to the left and your body positions the board to turn left, and vice versa.

- Description: Getting air — rider uses wake to get board in the air (off the water)
- Category: Beginner
- Point Value: 90

Tip on performing this trick: Approach the wake at a moderate speed, hitting it square and head on. Keep your knees slightly bent. As you go up the wake, straighten your knees a little to get some spring — and try not to flatten out the board until after you have taken off and are about ready to land. This is called edging through the wake and it is critical to improving the height of your jumps.

- Description: Bunny hop—getting air without using a wake
- Category: Beginner
- Point Value: 125

Tip on performing this trick: With this trick it is important to load the tow line with a little resistance from the handle and a downward push on the tail of the board. This combined force generates the pop known as a bunny hop.

- Description: Surface 180—board changes direction (back-front/front-back)
- Category: Beginner
- Point Value: 125

Tip on performing this trick: Surface 180s are a fun trick to learn as you become familiar with riding your board. Left-foot-forward boarders rotate to the left, righties to the right. Try to place your weight over the center of the board. In one smooth motion, swing the board around, leading with your rear foot. Once you are in the 180-degree position, place more weight on the tip to allow the board to track for stability. To get back around, do the same thing from back to front.

A Short History of Wakeboarding

Wakeboarding has evolved from many different forms at different times to become what it is today: the fastest-growing water sport in America.

For decades, surfing has been a favorite sport of beach dwellers. And in that time, historians recall surfers being towed with a ski rope behind a boat — sometimes even from the shoreline by a truck. Then surfers began using shorter boards. In 1985 a San Diego surfer named Tony Finn developed the Skurfer — a hybrid of a water ski and a surfboard. It looked like a little surfboard and was pulled by a boat while the rider performed surf-style carving moves on the wake. This riding style evokes visions of snowboarding and skateboarding, with a bit of waterskiing mixed in. Riders stood anywhere on these boards since there were no straps or bindings.

In the summer of 1985, footstraps were added to the Skurfer. What makes this interesting is that this innovation came simultaneously from two people who had no idea what the other was doing. Finn added the straps to his Skurfer, while Jimmy Redmon in Austin, Texas, added straps to his Redline design water-ski board, which was a smaller version of a surfboard, causing raves in Texas. The significance of footstraps can't be overestimated in the evolution of wakeboarding. Footstraps allowed people do big air moves, taking the sport to something more than surfing. Something dynamic and free-flowing — more like snowboarding and waterskiing.

Then Herb O'Brien, a successful businessman in water skiing and owner of H.O. Sports, started tinkering with the newly developed boards. He introduced the first compression-molded, neutral-buoyancy wakeboard, the Hyperlite. This innovation sparked the massive growth of what today is known as wakeboarding. (The term skiboarding stuck around for a few years, but wakeboarding ultimately became the official name of this sport.) The Hyperlite's neutral buoyancy allowed the rider to submerge it for easy deepwater starts.

O'Brien continued to refine the wakeboard, giving it a thin profile that would carve the water like a slalom ski. He added phasers (large dimples on the bottom), which broke up water adhesion and gave the board a quicker, loose feel and softer landings from wake jumps. The thin shape, neutral buoyancy, and phasers were features made possible by the compression-molding process. Following the lead of H.O. Sports, other board companies started manufacturing wakeboards as well.

As the sport grew, the boards continued to get better. The first Hyperlites, designed and built in 1990, had the overall shape of a surfboard with an obvious tip and tail. In 1993, Redmon researched and developed the twin-tip design — a symmetrical shape that has become today's standard in the sport. Twin-tip boards have a fin on both ends, allowing a centered stance that results in equal performance whether the wakeboarder rides in the forward or switch-stance position.

The World Wakeboard Association is the worldwide governing body of the sport. Redmon founded the

WWA in 1989 and is considered the guru of wake-boarding. He is responsible for developing the rules and formats to keep the integrity of the sport and the essence of wakeboarding in its present form.

The sport began to flourish professionally in 1992, when World Sports & Marketing, a Florida-based sports promoter and event organizer, began staging pro wake-board competitions. This gave wakeboarders a chance to compete professionally and earned them exposure on ESPN and later ESPN2.

The year 1998 saw the debut of a worldwide profes-sional series, the Wakeboard World Cup. It strings together the most prestigious contests in the world to crown a season champion. As wakeboarding enters the twenty-first century, the ultimate titles for any profes-sional rider are the Pro Wakeboard Tour, the Vans Triple Crown of Wakeboarding, and the Wakeboard World Cup.

Extreme Profile

Tony Alvarez
Trick Biking

Tony Alvarez has it all: success, money, and admirers. As a Disney stunt biker, he performs before big crowds.

Tony once lived to ride. It was his passion—the thing that drove him. It was his god. For a while he worked at DisneyWorld, performing for thousands. Now he does exhibitions around the world.

He says, "I got hired at DisneyWorld to do stunt shows. I was eighteen years old. I was riding in front of sixty-five thousand people a day. I was on national television. According to the world's point of view, I had it all together."

But he didn't. From his young teen days, his life had been a mess. He quit high school to do flatland freestyle trick biking. He began getting gigs and performing stunts in Miami Beach, Florida. Then at night he'd hit the parties and use drugs. It was wearing him down.

He recalls, "I was just so unstable. It was driving me nuts. I'd get kicked out of my mom's house, go to live with my dad, get kicked out of my dad's house, go to my friend's house, then get kicked out of my friend's house. And in my frame of mind, all of these people were nuts. That's when I really started searching for other things, which led to becoming involved in New Age stuff—parapsychology, metaphysics, meditation—things I totally didn't understand. But I thought it was something that maybe would help me out."

One day he met someone at a Miami restaurant. Tony says, "I met a girl at a restaurant, a born-again Christian. She invited me to church. At that point God had prepared my heart, and I went to church and just gave my life to Christ."

Tony found real acceptance at church. He stopped living the extreme life while doing his extreme sport. A few years later, he married Amber, the girl he'd met in the restaurant. Tony recalls, "This was a new horizon for me. I'd never experienced anything like this. My spirit just shot through the roof."

What kinds of changes came into his life? Amber says, "When he became a born-again Christian, he stopped doing the drugs, stopped pornography, stopped having sex with everything, stopped the promiscuous lifestyle, and just took his hands to the plow and gave his life to the Lord."

Now Tony takes his BMX gear on the road to tell others about Christ and his changed life. There's a ministry called Celestial Style, through which he travels the world, doing his bike tricks and preaching Jesus.

Tony says, "The things that I faced when I was younger are a lot of things that kids are facing today—drugs, a broken family, insecurity, a lack of hope in school. They don't know if they want to pursue school. Nobody's offering them anything. There are no role models out there. We want to bring the message that a personal relationship with Jesus Christ will change your life forever. That's what it boils down to. That's the message we're trying to get across.

If you'd like to contact Tony, check out his website at www.tonyalvarez.org.

lyndyn Ringrose:
Surfer for the Savior

onal	Age: 29
	Wife: Kate
	Vehicle: Ancient diesel van

fing Highlight: 1999 Ranking: 24

e of Glyndyn's quiver of surfboards: a six-foot bubble ish, three longer boards (6'2", 6'4", and 6'7") from a range of shapers—Pete Lascelles, Cordell Miller, Mark Phipps, Phil Grace, and Glyndyn himself. Glyndyn is a professional shaper/designer at home in Phillip Island, Australia, but chooses not to shape many boards himself while on tour, feeling that without constant shaping, consistency falls away.

e of Glyndyn's body: Fit and (mostly) healthy. Glyndyn stretched the medial ligament in his right knee at Pipe ast year but came back without any chronic problems. He has a developing case of surfer's ear, resulting in occasional ear infections.

all: Glyndyn is straight up in admitting that 2000 was a ough year for him. Competition seedings paired him regularly against Rob Machado, whose return to serious contender form left Glyndyn on the wrong side of several very narrow wins. But as a committed Christian, he is unlikely to collapse in despair as a result of losing. He remains confident in his free-surfing skills but wonders if he can regain some rhythm—and, perhaps, favor with the udging panels—quickly enough to get another World Championship Tour (WCT) seeding for 2002. He will be one of several top pros whose last months of the competitive year will be spent in a chase for requalifying points.

A wave looms up before Glyndyn Ringrose. He climbs it on his board, then slides down the backside, still flat on his board. No, that wasn't the one.

He watches the waves, studies them to find just the right swell and slope to indicate the right curl, the right pipe.

Then he sees it. The wave is coming in fast. He darts toward it, climbs it, and then he's on his board. The wave curls above and around him. He's in the pipeline. It's perfect. He surfs the wave, moving up and down on the board, performing tricks, amazing the crowd.

Competitions like this one are tough. The forty-three surfers competing against Glyndyn today are good. But Glyndyn is one of the best, and he knows his business.

Glyndyn Ringrose is one of the top surfers in the world today, ranking in the top forty-four for several years now. At age ten, he began surfing in Australia—and dreaming of becoming a pro.

"I've always had a natural attraction to surfing," he explains. "My parents were missionaries, and we grew up on the Solomon Islands. My brother and I caught our first waves standing in our dugout canoes. When we moved to Australia and saw real surfing for the first time, we were stoked. We instantly connected with it."

He first began to enjoy surfing when his family moved to Phillip Island, where he learned some of the great moves he's capable of today. He says, "My competitive career had just been building up from Phillip Island boardriders contests, to state titles, the national circuit, and then to the World Qualifying Series. I can remember thinking about how good it would be to compete on the world tour when I was a grommet. But, while I had the desire, I never really thought that I would actually do it."

Glyndyn is grateful to be living a childhood dream. But the life of a world-class competitive surfer isn't easy. "Competing on the World Qualifying Series has been a real challenge in the last couple of years," he says. "I've really needed God's help to get me through it. Just getting [travel] visas usually takes a small miracle! Then you travel to strange destinations that you have never been to before. You arrive in the middle of the night with a piece of paper with the name of a beach on it. There are different languages to come to terms with, different cultures, laws, and religions. It's a lot to deal with, especially when you are traveling on your own. On top of that, I usually have to do well in a contest to make enough money to get me to the next destination. It takes a lot of faith, and a lot of commitment."

Glyndyn's wife, Kate, is a real help to him on these trips. She goes almost everywhere with him and is his top cheerleader and supporter. Glyndyn says, "Kate plays an enormous part in my career; she keeps me on track. We pray together, which strengthens our faith so we can witness to others. As a hairdresser, she supports our ministry."

Glyndyn likes the fact that there are other Christians on the tour, people such as C. J. Hobgood and Tim Curran. They all fellowship regularly and reach out to their fellow competitors, seeking to get the gospel out to the surfing world, a world in which partying, drinking, and drugs are commonplace. When young admirers ask him for tips on surfing, he can't help but offer advice that will point them in the direction of Christ. He often says, "Keep on trying. Don't give up. Remember to sleep well, eat well, and keep fit. Start each day with God, talk to him, make him your personal friend."

On the World Championship Tour, Glyndyn competes against forty-three other men for top ranks, money, and prizes. Eleven women also compete on the tour. The tour started this year at Jeffrey's Bay in South Africa, which sports some of the best waves in the world, and continues on from there.

You can be sure that Glyndyn will be among them and shooting for the top of the wave, giving glory to God all along the way.

Trials on Tour

BY ROB SCHOEDEL

Surfing small waves is my weakness, and most of the Brazilian competitions are held in small waves. Sometimes, I was ripped out of the water in the competitions over there. I would go out in a heat and do everything I could, but my best just wasn't good enough. I might get through one heat, but then I'd lose the next one.

When you're on a losing streak, you get ripped apart psychologically. In one contest, I paddled out feeling totally defeated before the heat even started. I couldn't even figure out where I was going to sit to catch waves. I was an emotional wreck, and my confidence was at an all-time low.

All these things just kept building up and building up. I felt really lost. I was missing my wife and was really lonely. I lost in my first heat, and then as I was leaving the water this guy came up to me and said, "You haven't paid for the contest." I had paid, but he was demanding I pay another hundred dollars for the entry fee. I only had about three hundred dollars at this stage, and I was trying to explain that I needed all my money to get home. He still demanded that I pay it, so I gave him the money. I was worn out. I just wanted to go home.

I have learned to accept that uncertainty is a part of life. There will always be lows you need to endure, but it's faith that gets you through them. I didn't do very well in the first three contests last year, when I went to Brazil again. Suddenly I felt all this pressure on me again and was starting to get depressed. When I got to Rio for the fourth contest, I was praying, "Please help me here, Lord."

Before the contest I was feeling really good, and then my ear blocked up with water. I was in a hospital getting my ear flushed out two hours before my first heat. I got back with just enough time to paddle out for my heat. Again I just asked God to calm me down and set me straight. I ended up making the final — it just felt like a miracle.

In everything I do, I know in the back of my mind that God is in control. The Bible promises that "God won't test us beyond what we can bear." I get great comfort from knowing that. I used to have a lot of anxiety about traveling, but now I've learned to trust God. Sometimes I'd like to live safely in my comfort zone like everyone else. But your faith doesn't develop if you never step out of your comfort zone. Neither does your surfing. It's just incredible what faith can accomplish.

It's only through faith and by trusting in Jesus that I am where I am today. I'm still searching, reading the Bible, and growing. I've had some great experiences along the way, met some great people, and surfed my share of awesome waves. But the thing that gives me the most joy out of all of it is my faith in Jesus.

6

Tom Kipp: Motorcycler on the Move

Personal	Age: 32 Marital Status: Single
AMA Accomplishments	1992—AMA 600 SuperSport Championship 1994—AMA 750 SuperSport Title 1995—AMA 750 SuperSport Title 1999—AMA 750 SuperSport Title (Retired in 2001)

*T*he first thing you notice is the noise—the whining and roar of the machines as they rev. Then, with a little touch on the throttle, the 750cc motorcycles seem to come alive. When the flag waves, the racers are off.

For the first two laps, no one can match Tom Kipp's pace. His big Suzuki isn't well suited to the track, but he has managed to qualify for the first-row position.

The pack comes around the first turn, engines roaring, the noise rising into the air like a great crescendo in the *1812 Overture.* Haven't heard that one? Listen to it. It's got cannons.

These machines sound like big guns. And they're fast, sleek, and tough. Sit on one of these bulls, and you'll feel the adrenaline pumping through your heart. On the straightaways, you reach 180 mph, a horrid speed, with no protective metal around you.

Racing at this pace, your heart pounds more than 180 beats a minute (normal is about 70), which is three beats a second. You can feel it in your chest like a little version of that 750cc engine.

It's the third lap now, and Kipp maintains the lead, trying his hardest to create a gap while his tires are cool. Soon, though, the tires are heating up and feel almost stuck to the pavement, despite whipping around turns at just under 100 mph.

Kipp is not worried about losing this race. Worries seem far away. The joy of simply riding—riding for his team, riding for fun, riding for God—is what matters to him.

It's sheer exhilaration.

Someone is behind him now, trying to pass. Kipp hunkers down, throttles the huge Suzuki that feels to him like a living, breathing dragon underneath him. He whips around turn six, straight ahead to victory.

Now that didn't seem hard, did it?

It probably didn't look that hard, but then Tom Kipp has been running these superbikes for many years.

Tom started riding motocross bikes at age six, and until he was fifteen, he was full-bore into it. He quit riding for about a year, then got a chance to get into a rider's school at Summit Point, West Virginia. There, he learned how to drive a Yamaha FJ 600. He loved it.

1990 was one of his best years. He says, "I was racing a Wiseco-sponsored Yamaha OWO1. We had a lot of good races that year. I led the Daytona 200, and man, that felt good, but the motor blew up. But I led a lot of races that year."

The year 1992 was even better. He won many races, including the AMA 600 SuperSport Championship. But his real goal was to move up to the 750cc class.

Tom suffered a major setback in 1993, crashing and breaking his leg. He found himself laid up at home with a huge cast. He was only twenty-four years old, and he lost his sponsor because of the injury. He recalls, "I broke my leg real bad. I couldn't ride for a while, but I still worked . . . for those guys [at Honda]. I mean I couldn't ride, but I did every promotional thing that I could. I wasn't contracted to them after 1993, and they didn't re-sign me because they were unsure of my leg and how long I would take to be back."

At that point, Tom began talking to another sponsor, Suzuki. He says, "I didn't have a ride for the next season, and it seemed that all the rides would be taken up by the time my leg healed completely. But I just kept training, like I knew that God had a plan for me. I knew that something would work out, so I trained really hard, with all of my heart. Ski [David Sadowski] told me that I should go with him to the Daytona tire tests in December. Most of the top teams were there (and

Race Preparation—Tom Kipp Style

By the time we go to a race, I already know what my game plan is. It does not do me any good to stew about it for those few short minutes before I go out on the track. The warm-up lap is plenty of time for me to put it all together and get refocused.

"Ray Plumb, with the help of HRC Japan, has been working really hard to come up with a solution for a clutch problem. It seems to be working well in recent races, so when I come back to the grid I am thinking first-lap strategy and what is the safest and quickest way to smoke everyone off the line.

"What really works well for me is to get as relaxed as possible, joke around with my mechanic, whatever. I just try to stay loose because you should already have it worked out in your mind as to what you're going to do, what your strategy is. There is no sense sitting there on the line just getting yourself all worked up. It's not going to do you any good. I come back from the warm-up lap, and the only thing I'm thinking is ... smoke 'em."

we hadn't been invited), but Ski and I drove there from Ohio. And when we showed up, they wouldn't let us in the gate!

"At that point, I realized I didn't have a whole lot of control over the situation anymore. It was a difficult time. I had to rely on God in many ways to get me through that. I grew a lot in that period and had a peace about how it would turn out." (Tom had made a Christian commitment two years earlier but admits, "I had not given my life over to the Lord.")

From then on, Jesus, not winning races, became Tom's top priority. But he was still as fierce a competitor as ever, as three more championships have shown.

He says, "I never doubted myself, but when I didn't have a ride, that was the only time I ever thought, 'Whoa, I don't know how much longer I am going to be able to do this.' I was kind of let down that Honda didn't stick with me, but I always knew that I could make it back. It was really hard to swallow, not having a ride, and everyone treating me like an unknown.

"But I made it through, and the ride with Suzuki was really good. I feel that I owe those guys a lot for believing in me. They worked really hard to provide me with good bikes, and to be competitive, and I was able to win the championship for them."

Brent Houston, a chaplain with Motor Racing Outreach (MRO), an organization committed to reaching auto, boat, and motorcycle racers for Christ, says Tom has a championship attitude as well: "After his accident, [Tom's] relationship with Jesus Christ changed. At that point, he wasn't afraid to stand up for his faith. Now he lives his faith day after day after day. It's visible on his face. He's always accessible to the fans, even after he has a rough day. A lot of the riders won't talk to fans after bad days, but Tom makes up for that."

Tom's aggressive yet skillful driving and winning personality will be missed on the tour, as he's now retired. But he is looking ahead more than he's looking back. He hasn't married yet, but there are many years ahead to think about that. He says, "In a competitive environment, a lot of things tend to take a back seat. I've made a lot of sacrifices in the way of my family and friends. That's tough sometimes. I feel as if God has given me an ability to ride motorcycles, and to do it well. I rode for Him as much as for any team owner, and that meant going all out for Him."

You can be sure Tom Kipp will continue to go all out for God in the days ahead, off the track or on it. We'll be looking for him!

References

"2000 Wakeboard World Cup Final Standings." Information at http://www.wakeworld.com/News/2000/StandingsWorldCup.asp.

Adams, Dean. "Tom Kipp Interview, 1993." Article at http://www.amasuperbike.com/tomkipp1993.htm

Baker, Robyne. "Rock Star," *Campus Life,* July/August 2000, p. 52.

Baker, Robyne. "Vertical Reality," *Sharing the Victory,* June-July 1999.

"Beginner Wakeboard Trick Descriptions." Information at http://www.wakeworld.com/tourney/trickdescprint.asp?TrickCat=Beginner.

Branon, Dave. "Racing Heat," *Sports Spectrum,* Racing 2000 issue, pp. 14–15.

Canavan, Todd. "Interview: AMA 750 Supersport Champion Tom Kipp." Article at http://www.motorcycle.com/mo/mcmail/kipp95.html.

Christian Surfers Australia, Member Interviews. "Glyndon Ringrose Top 44." Article at http://www.christiansurfers.org.au/member.html.

Demeo, Janey L. "Reaching for the Top," *Sports Spectrum*, June 2000, p. 6.

"Frequently Asked Questions and Answers on Wakeboarding." Information at http://www.wakeworld.com/FAQ/.

"Greg Albertyn to Retire." Article at http://www.supercross.com/homenews/albertyn_00.html.

Johnston, Andy. "Going All Out," *Sports Spectrum*, Racing 2000 issue, p. 27.

Kithcart, David. "The Best High of All: The Story of Jay Haizlip." http://www.cbn.com/CC/article/1,1183,PTID2546CHIDCIID137979,00.html.

"Making the Cut" (Pamphlet: In His Wakes, P.O. Box 1099, Keystone Heights, FL 32565). http://www.prowakeboardtour.com.

Moring, Mark. "Going to Extremes," *Campus Life*, January/February 1998.

Palmeri, Allen. "Extreme Honesty," *Sports Spectrum*, June/July 2000, 30–31.

Rielly, Stephen. "Ringrose Chases a Place among the Elite."

Schafer, Guy. "Noah Snyder: Surfer Gets Saved at the Ark." Article at http://www.christianity.com/CC/article/1,1183,PTID2546CHIDCIID135809,00.html

Schoedel, Rob. "Amateur Tournaments." Article at http://www.wakeworld.com/tourney/amateurevents.asp.

Stanley, Matt. "Katie Brown: Setting the Standard."

Swell Magazine. "The Magazine Contest Zone." http://www.swell.com/sw/content/mag/czone/scorecards/men/ringrose_glyndyn.jsp

"Team Suzuki's 250 AMA National Champion Greg Albertyn." Interview at http://www.supercross.com/interviews/albertyn00.html.

Thomas, Stephanie. "On the Road with Jesus." Article at http://www.christianity.com/CC/article/1,1183,PTID 2546 CHID CIID 137586,00.html

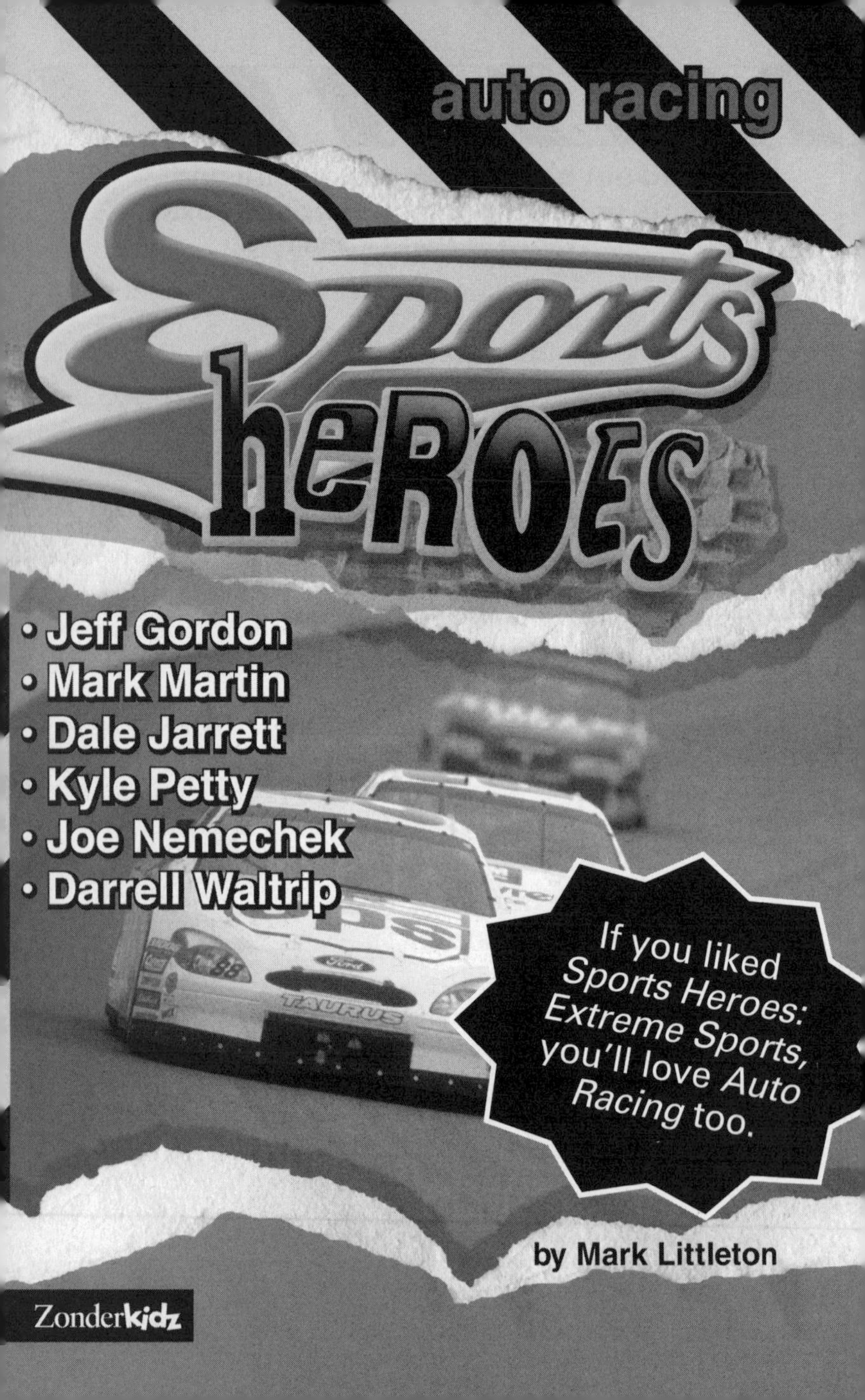
auto racing
Sports Heroes
• Jeff Gordon
• Mark Martin
• Dale Jarrett
• Kyle Petty
• Joe Nemechek
• Darrell Waltrip
If you liked Sports Heroes: Extreme Sports, you'll love Auto Racing too.
by Mark Littleton
Zonderkidz

JEFF GORDON:
Driving Like the Wind

Personal	Height: 5'7" Weight: 150
	Spouse: Brooke
	Birth date: August 4, 1971
	Hobbies: water skiing, video games
Contact	Jeff Gordon National Fan Club
	P.O. Box 515
	Williams, AZ 86046–0515
	520–635–5333
	Website: www.jeffgordon.com
NASCAR Facts	Car: #24, Chevy
	Sponsor: Du Pont
	Team: Hendrick Motorsports
	Crew Chief: Robbie Loomis

Photo by: Donald Miralle/Allsport

The year is 1997. The race, the Daytona 500. The announcer booms, "A million dollars, a mile away! Can anyone get by Jeff Gordon? He pulls them down the super stretch. Labonte looks inside, looks outside. No, it's Gordon in three!"

Back at Daytona, 1999. "Gordon is holding his line," the announcer says. "Earnhardt has to make the move. Nothing there down low. Gordon's car is glued to the bottom of the racetrack. Earnhardt can't do anything. Jeff Gordon wins the Daytona 500 for the second time!"

Daytona 1999 was one of Jeff Gordon's greatest races. Already one of the best NASCAR drivers of all time, the thirty-year-old speedster has many racing years and championships ahead of him. He will easily make the Hall of Fame. Being a championship driver is a long-time dream for Jeff. He started racing at age four—on his bicycle.

Jeff grew up a daredevil. He would try anything. His stepfather understood Jeff's need for speed. When young Jeff was four and a half years old, his stepfather walked into the house and said to the boy and his sister, "Come here. Look out the window."

Jeff ran to the window. His eyes sparkled as he saw two miniature racecars on a trailer. Jeff sprinted outside and checked over his new baby. Excited but terrified, he finally got into it and drove—like the wind.

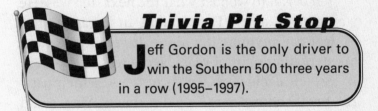

Trivia Pit Stop

Jeff Gordon is the only driver to win the Southern 500 three years in a row (1995–1997).

Soon, Jeff was winning races. By age eight, he was racing on the quarter-midget circuit, blowing by his opponents like they were stalled in rush-hour traffic.

But Jeff almost didn't make it to age eight. When he was only six, he had a frightening accident. He recalls, "I got into a crash in a quarter-midget car. I hit the wall and flipped upside down. My foot was wedged between the gas pedal and the frame rail, and I thought I broke my ankle. I was screaming. I thought after that day, *I'm never going to get back in a racecar*."

There was only one problem: Driving racecars was the only thing Jeff did well!

School? That was a bust. Other sports? He was too small. Musical instruments? Forget about it.

But racing? Man, could Jeff drive!

So he stuck with it. He celebrated his birthday every year at the racetrack. He won a national championship in 1979, at the age of eight, on his birthday weekend.

Then he won the national title again in 1981.

Jeff began to wonder what the next step was. He was getting older. He couldn't fit in a quarter-midget car anymore, let alone drive one. Besides, his stepfather's gift of years before was worn out.

So Jeff decided to try sprint cars, which pack 750 to 800 horsepower—on dirt tracks. Man, could they peel out! Soon, he was winning even more awards and honors.

Beyond the track, though, he was a shy boy who wondered if anyone noticed him.

"When I was at the racetrack, I felt comfortable," Jeff recalls. "But as soon as I left that racetrack, I was a very timid little boy who didn't excel at anything else."

He longed to run to the racetrack because that was where he did well. Nothing else seemed to work for him.

Jeff Gordon's teen years were tough. At times he ran with the wrong group of kids. But whether they were from the wrong crowd or the right crowd, few

NASCAR Starts Its Engines!

After World War II (1941–1945), car manufacturers began producing cars that were faster and sleeker than ever before. People wanted to race cars like these, vehicles similar to the ones they normally drove. They didn't want special racing cars like Formula 1 cars or the low-to-the-ground numbers you see in the Indianapolis 500. So, stock car racing was born. This brand of racing got its name because it featured cars normally kept in stock at car dealerships around the country.

In the late 1940s, various organizations were created to promote this new sport and keep it organized. These had acronyms like NCSCC, SCAR, NSCRA, USCRA, and NARL, with dozens of others in existence.

One man decided to bring order to this alphabet soup of confusion. Bill France Sr., known as Big Bill, gathered thirty-five important auto-racing people together in December 1947. Their goal: to create a national stock car racing body.

The group met for four days and came up with the name NASCAR—the National Association for Stock Car Auto Racing.

Pick up a copy today at your local bookstore!
Softcover 0-310-70292-5

We want to hear from you. Please send your comments about this book to us in care of the address below. Thank you.

Zonder**kidz**.

Grand Rapids, MI 49530
www.zonderkidz.com